# Ladybug Girl
## and
## Bumblebee Boy

by David Soman and Jacky Davis

Dial Books for Young Readers

# Ladybug Girl

and

## Bumblebee Boy

by David Soman and Jacky Davis

Dial Books for Young Readers

For Benjamin and Netanya, Super-Heroes

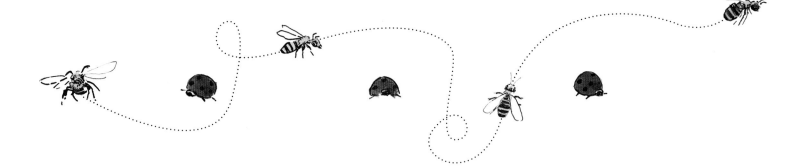

DIAL BOOKS FOR YOUNG READERS
A division of Penguin Young Readers Group
Published by The Penguin Group
Penguin Group (USA) Inc., 375 Hudson Street, New York, NY 10014, U.S.A.
Penguin Group (Canada), 90 Eglinton Avenue East, Suite 700, Toronto, Ontario, Canada M4P 2Y3 (a division of Pearson Penguin Canada Inc.)
Penguin Books Ltd, 80 Strand, London WC2R 0RL, England
Penguin Ireland, 25 St. Stephen's Green, Dublin 2, Ireland (a division of Penguin Books Ltd)
Penguin Group (Australia), 250 Camberwell Road, Camberwell, Victoria 3124, Australia (a division of Pearson Australia Group Pty Ltd)
Penguin Books India Pvt Ltd, 11 Community Centre, Panchsheel Park, New Delhi - 110 017, India
Penguin Group (NZ), 67 Apollo Drive, Rosedale, North Shore 0632, New Zealand (a division of Pearson New Zealand Ltd)
Penguin Books (South Africa) (Pty) Ltd, 24 Sturdee Avenue, Rosebank, Johannesburg 2196, South Africa
Penguin Books Ltd, Registered Offices: 80 Strand, London WC2R 0RL, England

Text copyright © 2009 by Jacky Davis
Pictures copyright © 2009 by David Soman
All rights reserved

The publisher does not have any control over and does not assume any
responsibility for author or third-party websites or their content.
Designed by Teresa Dikun and Jasmin Rubero
Text set in Aunt Mildred
Manufactured in China on acid-free paper

1 3 5 7 9 10 8 6 4 2

Library of Congress Cataloging-in-Publication Data
Soman, David.
Ladybug Girl and Bumblebee Boy / by David Soman and Jacky Davis.
p.    cm.
Summary: Lulu, dressed as Ladybug Girl, goes to the playground and
makes new friends, including Bumblebee Boy.
ISBN 978-0-8037-3339-8
Special Markets ISBN 978-0-8037-3558-3
[1. Imagination—Fiction. 2. Play—Fiction. 3. Friendship—Fiction.]
I. Davis, Jacky, date. II. Title.
PZ7.S696224Lad 2009
[E]—dc22
2008001719

"Ladybug Girl is ready to play!" says Lulu.
She has been waiting **forever** to go to her favorite playground—the one with the **twisty slide** and the **bouncy dinosaurs.**

Her mama grabs Bingo's leash and says,
"All right, let's go!"

Ladybug Girl leaps over sidewalk cracks
that are as big as canyons.
When she sees Mrs. Robbins carrying her groceries,
Ladybug Girl swoops over to help.
The bag is as heavy as a boulder,
but it isn't a problem for
Ladybug Girl.

And Ladybug Girl can
count **really** high.
She counts mailbox after mailbox
after mailbox,
all the way up to **infinity**.
Bingo sniffs everything.

When they get to the playground, it is full of kids.
While Bingo settles into his spot under a bench,
Lulu looks around for someone to play with.

She sees Sam, from her music class.
He's playing by himself in the sandbox.
"Hi, Sam," she says.
   "Hi, Lulu," he says back.
"Want to play with me?"
   "Sure. What do you want to play?" asks Lulu.

"Diggers, of course!" says Sam.
Lulu has never really liked
playing diggers. She doesn't like
getting sand in her boots.

"How about monkeys?"
In a flash Lulu is
hanging from the jungle gym.
**"Monkeys is the best!"**
Lulu yells.
"No, I don't like that,"
says Sam.

Lulu watches Sam run off to the big castle.
*Well, maybe we could play castle,* Lulu thinks.
Being a princess wouldn't be so bad.
But Sam is standing at the bottom of the castle,
and that's not where she usually plays.
"Why are you down **there**?" Lulu asks, puzzled.
"Don't you think playing on the **top** is better?"

When Sam doesn't answer, Lulu says,
"Never mind, I know the perfect thing for us to do!
The seesaw!" She runs over and
sits down on one side of the seesaw

and waits.
And waits.
Sam just stands there, not getting on.
The other side is high and empty
while she is stuck on the ground.

Lulu and Sam glare at each other. Neither one of them says anything.
    Then Lulu sputters,
"You don't want to do anything I want to do!"
"And you don't want to do
        what I want!" Sam grumbles.

Lulu's cheeks are getting hot.
She is very frustrated! Why doesn't Sam want to play?
She definitely didn't have this problem
on the way to the playground, when she was
Ladybug Girl!
It was easy to have fun then.
Maybe she should just go play
by herself.

And then Lulu has an idea.
She takes a deep breath and says,
"Do you want to play Ladybug Girl with me?"
"Ladybug Girl? How do you play that?"
asks Sam.

"I'll show you!" she says.
"Ladybug Girl has superpowers!
I can fly and I'm superstrong!"

"Superpowers?"
Sam is very interested.

"And who can I be?" he asks.

"Well, you sort of look like a bee . . ." says Lulu.

"A bee? Yeah! A bee can fly!

And he will sting people if they bother him!

I need a stinger . . ." says Sam.

He sees a stick and picks it up.

"I'm Bumblebee Boy!"
Sam declares.
"And I'm Ladybug Girl!"
yells Lulu.

"Nothing can stop us!"

Ladybug Girl and Bumblebee Boy zoom around the playground looking to help anyone in trouble. A squirrel scampers by Bingo. "Oh no!" yells Bumblebee Boy. "That Scary Monster is trying to get your dog! He needs our help right away!"

"We're coming, Bingo!"
says Bumblebee Boy.
They bravely charge forward.
The Scary Monster is no match for their
superpowers and leaps away.

"We did it!
   We saved Bingo!
Are you okay?" asks
   Ladybug Girl.
      Bingo wags his tail.

Then **Bumblebee Boy** runs toward the swings.

"Watch how high I can fly!" he yells.

"I can fly high too!" **Ladybug Girl** says, running behind him.

They are soon whipping through the air.

They flap their wings harder and harder.

They are so high, they can almost touch a cloud.

"Look!" says Ladybug Girl, waving toward the tire swing.
"There's a Mean Robot! It's going to crush the playground!
We need to stop it!"
They rush over to the Mean Robot. Ladybug Girl grabs on,
and jumps on top of its head! Bumblebee Boy stings it
with his stinger again and again.
"This will teach you
not to mess with
Bumblebee Boy!"

"And Ladybug Girl!"

Feeling rather proud for saving the playground and probably the whole town, **Ladybug Girl** and Bumblebee Boy decide to have a parade on the bouncy dinosaurs.

It is a **very** important celebration.
A crowd gathers to watch the parade.
People cheer and throw flowers at them.

Two girls who are watching them come over.

"Can we play with you?" asks Marley. "I can be Butterfly Girl!"

"No!" says Kiki. "We already decided I'm Butterfly Girl!

You can be Dragonfly Girl!"

Ladybug Girl and Bumblebee Boy

look at them.

"If we're going to play together,"
says Ladybug Girl, "we don't fight each other."
"Yeah, we work together to fight bad guys,
like that Giant Snake over there!"
says Bumblebee Boy, pointing at the twisty slide.
Ladybug Girl adds,
"And Dragonfly Girl can breathe fire!"
"Fire?! I'm Dragonfly Girl!" agrees Marley.

As **Dragonfly Girl** breathes fire,
**Ladybug Girl** yells,

"Watch out, you big Giant Snake! Here comes the Bug Squad!"

Later, when it's time to go, Lulu says, "It was fun playing together."

"Do you want to play Bug Squad tomorrow?" asks Sam.

"Definitely! Because Ladybug Girl and Bumblebee Boy

can do anything!"

"Mama," asks Lulu as they head home, "can we get wings for Bingo?"